P9-DMQ-964

WITHDRAWN

Shaggy Dogs, Waggy Dogs

by Patricia Hubbell

illustrated by Donald Wu

Marshall Cavendish Children

Text copyright © 2011 by Patricia Hubbell
Illustrations copyright © 2011 by Donald Wu

All rights reserved

Marshall Cavendish Corporation, 99 White Plains Road, Tarrytown, NY 10591
www.marshallcavendish.us/kids

Library of Congress Cataloging-in-Publication Data
Hubbell, Patricia.
Shaggy dogs, waggy dogs / by Patricia Hubbell ; illustrated by Donald Wu.—1st ed.
p. cm.
Summary: Although dogs enjoy riding in trucks and romping in parks, their favorite activity is loving you.
ISBN 978-0-7614-5957-6 (hardcover) — ISBN 978-0-7614-6064-0 (ebook)
[1. Stories in rhyme. 2. Dogs—Fiction.] I. Wu, Donald, ill. II. Title.
PZ8.3.H848Sh 2011
[E]—dc22
2010044927

The illustrations are rendered in a mixed medium of colored pencils over acrylic on illustration board.
Book design by Anahid Hamparian
Editor: Marilyn Brigham

Printed in China (E)
First edition
10 9 8 7 6 5 4 3 2 1

For all of our dogs, past and present,
and especially for wonderful Cindy, our first Labrador
—P. H.

For Chip and Chessy
—D. W.

Shaggy dogs. Waggy dogs.

Pencil-thin and saggy dogs.

Country dogs.

City dogs.

Itty-bitty pretty dogs.

Shy dogs.

Bold dogs.

Won't-do-as-they're-told dogs.

Dogs in packs and
dogs alone.

Puppy dogs and dogs full grown.

Dogs can find your missing ball.

Give you kisses if you fall.

Take you for a long, long walk.

Listen to you when you talk.

Dogs can fetch your shoes and socks.

Bury bones. Dig up rocks.

Dogs romp and race in doggy parks.

They fill the air with yips and barks.

Dogs gulp and gobble when they eat.

They'll do a trick
to get a treat.

Dogs like to curl up
in your lap
and take a cozy,
snoozy nap.

Dogs comfort you
when you feel sick.

They're happy when you throw a stick.

With dirty paws and
mud-caked nose,
they jump up on your
nice, clean clothes.

Dogs ride in trucks. They ride in cars.

Some dogs are famous TV stars.

A team of dogs can pull a sled.

Dogs warm your feet when you're in bed.

Of all the things a dog can do—
its favorite thing is . . . loving YOU!